4/11

0294352

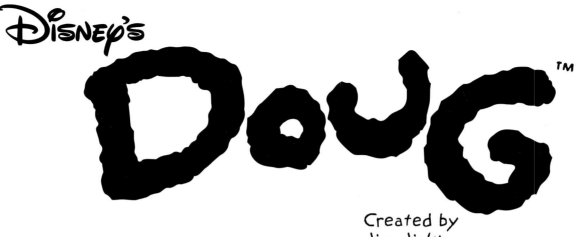

Disney's Doug ™

Created by Jim Jinkins

Doug Makes the Team

Story by Nancy Krulik

Illustrated by Matthew C. Peters, Jeffrey Nodelman, Vinh Truong, Brian Donnelly, Miriam Katin

Doug Makes the Team is hand-illustrated by the same Grade-A-Quality Jumbo artists who bring you *Disney's Doug*, the television series.

NEW YORK

Original characters for "The Funnies" developed by Jim Jinkins and Joe Aaron.

Copyright © 1998 by Disney Enterprises, Inc.

All rights reserved. No part of this book may be reproduced or transmitted in any form or by any means, electronic or mechanical, including photocopying, recording, or by any information storage and retrieval system, without written permission from the publisher. For information address Disney Press, 114 Fifth Avenue, New York, New York 10011-5690.

Printed in Singapore.

First Edition
1 3 5 7 9 10 8 6 4 2

The artwork for this book is prepared using watercolor.
The text for this book is set in 18-point New Century Schoolbook.

Library of Congress Catalog Card Number: 98-85316

ISBN: 0-7868-3193-6

For more Disney Press fun, visit www.DisneyBooks.com

Doug Funnie

Skeeter Valentine

Beebe Bluff

Doug's World

Roger Klotz

Porkchop

Patti Mayonnaise

The school gym was buzzing. Everyone was signing up for after-school activities.

"Honk-honk! It's the kazoo team for me," Skeeter declared.

"I'm going out for the soccer team. This year we're going to make it to the Tri-County play-offs," Patti said proudly.

"My after-school activity is counting my money," Roger boasted. He turned to Doug and added, "Hey, Funnie. I hear the Losers Club is looking for a new president."

Doug ignored Roger. "I'm with you, Patti," he said.

Patti looked surprised. "You mean you're going out for the soccer team, too?"

Doug would join *any* team with Patti on it—even the kazoo team! He smiled at her and said, "Uh. Well. Yeah. Soccer. Sure, Patti."

Porkchop and Doug walked to tryouts. Porkchop thought his best pal looked a little nervous.

Roger yelled from the stands, "Hey, Funnie, be careful. Somebody may want to use your head for a ball!"

Porkchop barked at Roger. Doug wondered if he'd made a big mistake.

Coach Spitz blew his whistle. The players lined up. They dribbled the ball around a set of cones.

Doug started out okay but when he checked to see if Patti was watching . . . *splat!* Doug tripped over a cone and fell headfirst into it.

"Oh, brother! What a conehead!" Roger guffawed.

The next day Coach Spitz announced the names of the kids who'd made the team. Roger laughed when he saw Doug in the crowd. "What are you doing here, Funnie?" he asked. "This isn't the list of kids who made it into clown school!"

Doug slumped and walked away. As he left, he could hear the names of the players being called out. "Studebaker, Chalky. Mayonnaise, Patti. Funnie, Doug."

"Funnie, Doug? I mean . . . Doug Funnie." Doug's face brightened. "Hey, that's me!"

Doug couldn't believe it! He made the team!

He imagined himself playing in a World Cup game. He raced down the field, never once losing control of the ball. He slammed the ball toward the goal. The goalie caught the ball, but Doug had kicked it so hard, it hurled the goalie right through the goal for a score!

"Oh, Doug," Patti cheered. "You're so . . . soccery!"

The crowd roared. "Doug-ie! Doug-ie! Doug-ie!"

"What position are you going to play, Doug?" Skeeter asked his best friend.

Doug shook his head. "Gee, I don't know." He turned toward Coach Spitz. "What position am I, Coach?"

"Well, Funnie, I tried you at center, wing, and goalie," Coach Spitz said. "But I think the best spot for you is on the sidelines. Every team needs a mascot, and I nominate you."

Coach Spitz handed Doug a huge papier-mâché head. It looked like Beebe Bluff with mumps.

Doug was humiliated. But before he could say anything Patti walked over. "I think it's great that you're going to be the mascot, Doug. Somebody's got to lead the cheers for the team. It's a big job."

That settled it. If Patti thought it was a good idea, then Doug would be the best mascot ever!

Later, Doug tried stuffing the giant Beebe head into a grocery bag, but it wouldn't fit. He had no choice but to wear the head home.

Walking in the giant head wasn't easy. Doug could barely see through the tiny eyeholes. *Slam!* Doug collided with a lamppost and landed in a trash can! This mascot thing was not starting out well.

As soon as Doug got home he raced up the stairs and took off his costume. Porkchop took one look at the giant Beebe head and dove for cover.

"I know how you feel, Porkchop," Doug groaned.

All week long, even as he was practicing his mascot routines, Doug tried to forget about Saturday's soccer game. He hoped Saturday would never come. But of course it did. Right after Friday.

At the field, Doug could hear Roger talking on the phone about his money. Doug hoped Roger wouldn't notice him. But it's tough *not* to notice a kid wearing a giant Beebe Bluff head.

But Roger didn't say anything nasty. He was laughing too hard!

The whistle blew. The center forward kicked the ball to Patti. She kicked the soccer ball into the cage. "Goal!" Beebe Bluff Middle School had the lead. Doug jumped up and down with excitement. He landed in a big mud puddle.

"Hey, watch what you do with that costume," the real Beebe Bluff shouted from the bleachers.

By the end of the first half, the score was tied.

Patti played her heart out in the second half. But by the final quarter the score was still tied. Patti got control of the ball. Suddenly, her foot slid over it. Patti fell, and she didn't get up.

Patti limped off the field. Coach Spitz took a look at her ankle. "It's just a sprain, Mayonnaise," he told her. "Get up and walk it off!"

Patti winced in pain. "I can't, Coach. I'm really hurt."

"Oh, for the love of Peat Moss!" shouted Coach Spitz.
"Who else do I have?" he asked looking down his roster.
"How about Benge, Connie?"
   "Connie's got the flu," Patti said.
   "How about Beaumont, Skunky?"
   "Skunky doesn't believe in sweating," Patti replied.

Doug raced to the bench. "Patti, are you okay?" he asked with concern.

Patti's face brightened. "How about Doug?" she asked.

Doug didn't think it was a good idea. But Roger did.

"Yeah! Put Funnie in!" Roger said. "We need a few laughs in this game."

Patti ignored Roger. "Come on. You can do it, Doug. I know you can."
Doug had never turned Patti down before. He wasn't about to start
now. "Put me in, Coach," Doug said, ignoring Roger's guffaws. "I'm ready
to play!"

"That's wonderful, Doug!" Patti cheered. "You'll be great. I know it."

"Maybe they should change this game from soccer to sucker," Roger shouted.

Doug tried to keep his eye on the ball but everyone was moving so fast! Suddenly, it flew right at him. . . .

Doug didn't have time to think so he used his head instead. *Slam!* The ball sailed toward the goal. The Medulla goalie reached up to catch it and . . .

. . . *whoosh!* It flew right past him!

"Yea, Doug!" the crowd roared.

"That's the best goal ever!" shouted Patti.

Even Roger was impressed. "Wow, Funnie! You really did it!"

And this time, it was for real.